Mulogo's Treatise on Wizardry

Being a Succinct Guide to a Magician's Survival in a World of Frequently Misguided but Well-Intentioned Knights, Wise but Often Hungry Dragons, Hordes of Rampaging Extradimensional Interlopers, Treacherous Backstabbing Rogues, Far-Reaching Nefarious Plots, and Random Calamity Brought Forth by Sorcerous Error[1]

Joseph J. Bailey
Scrivener

Scribe's Notes:

1. *A Wizard's Guide to Survival in a World Where People Want to Kill You and Take Your Stuff*[2]
2. *That's better.*

Scribe's Note:

1. *For the sake of the greater macroverse, I truly hope there is no resemblance. One Mulogo is far too many.*

Author's Note:

This brief, mildly amusing treatise is intended for people who enjoy short, fun reads.

If you do not enjoy things that are short or fun, this book is not for you.

That is not to say, however, that people who enjoy rather long-winded non-humorous lexicons, wandering interlocutions, and convoluted phraseologies will not find a modicum of levity within this otherwise very concise and to the point but largely farcical guide making light of wizardly conventions within the larger fantasy tradition, assorted related communities and offshoots, and various cultural derivatives.

Wizard's Note:

For those who are wizards, this tome will appear as it is and as it is intended.

For non-wizards, this treatise will appear to be a brief but thorough guide to trimming nose hairs.[1]

Scribe's Notes:

1. *Mulogo is a crotchety old curmudgeon. His cynicism and admonishments come from a good place.*[2]
2. *Mulogo's rather skewed sentiments are not representative of those of all wizards.*

To those who believe,
but, more importantly, to those who do not.

Magic is dangerous. Your choices are not.
(Or they shouldn't be.)

- Mulogo
Master of the Greatest Mysteries

Table of Contents

About Mulogo (An Introduction of Sorts)

Mulogo is one of the greatest wizards of his Age[1].

His fame spread far and wide after the publication of his magnum opus *Codependent Arising and Generation of Life, Magic, and the Real,* a grimoire outlining the simultaneous expression and interdependency of life, magic, and everything as originating from the universal primordial potential.

Still a young wizard at the time of the grand unified theory's publication, amidst the uproarious accolades and fame, Mulogo became a target for numerous nefarious plots, waves of unexpected violence from extradimensional entities, myriad manipulative power-seekers, gads of greedy ne'er-do-wells, and many more who interfered with his ever finding a moment to take a bite or a drink in peace, much less a nap.

Fortunately for Ea'ae[3], this crucible forged Mulogo into the wizard he is today: an archmage of unequaled stature[5], grand vision[6], indomitable will[7], and unending desire for relentless self-improvement and ultimate survival[8].

This brief treatise provides a concise summary in plain language[9] for any wizards who wish to have a guide to survival in an often harsh world and who may want to follow in his vaunted footsteps[10].

– Ludaceous Vaer Mordicanum, Scribe, Lesser Under Understudy, Apprentice Wizard 3rd Order, Gofer 2nd Class, Semi-Rebellious Sycophant, Assistant Baker and Order Clerk, and Yes-Man

Scribe's notes:

1. *Or any Age if you ask him.[2]*
2. *I try to ask him as little as possible.*

10

3. *Or unfortunately depending on your view.*[4]
4. *I will remain silent on this issue for the nonce.*
5. *For those who are even aware he still lives.*
6. *For those he is not berating, that is to say, never me.*
7. *Especially with regard to voicing his opinion to his limited audience... most especially me.*
8. *I.e. definitely paranoid.*
9. *Arcane formulae are available in separate tome for those who wish to see metamagical proof through his myriad labyrinthine ratiocinative permutations.*
10. *The Light help us all!*

So You Want to Be a Wizard?

I have had my homes razed, raided and burned to the ground, my towers gutted, marauded, and blasted, and my castles pillaged, defiled, and demolished.

I have been imprisoned in the Astral Plane, entombed in stone, had my spirit bound within a phylactery, and had my mind trapped within a crystal prism.

I have been held for ransom by bandits, robbed by nobility, and dispossessed by extradimensional thieves.

I have been threatened, cajoled, berated, cursed (both literally and actually), abused, and blackmailed.

I have been stabbed, bludgeoned, whipped, tortured, burned, shocked, flayed, and worse.[1]

I have been possessed, mind-controlled, robbed of my body and volition, and rendered incorporeal.

I have been turned into a newt, transmogrified into a frog, changed into a toad, and transformed into creatures slimier still.[2]

I have been charmed, bewitched, hexed, ensorcelled, enchanted, mesmerized, spellbound, and let's not even talk about what happened while I was under the influence of hostile supernatural entities and agents.

I have been abandoned by friends, forgotten by allies, scorned by compatriots, and turned upon by companions.

I have had intimates taken, comrades killed, family members persecuted, and kith imprisoned.

I have fought with incomprehensible daemons face to face, been engulfed by dragons' raging hellfires, clashed with greater Powers, and been laid low by alien intelligences.

I have been trapped within the bowels of forgotten ruins, lost within haunted crypts, striven through extradimensional labyrinths, delved over and through the hearts of uncharted planets, and foundered within the darkest and deepest wilds.

I have had my identity erased, my memories taken, my will sapped, and my spirit broken.

And these were on some of my better days.

I am a wizard.

Are you sure you want to be one?[3]

Scribe's note:

1. *But yet, no matter how pleasant the imagery, Mulogo is still with us.*
2. *Also some less slimy. It varies.*
3. *Not many wizards have been as fortunate as Mulogo.*

The Wizard's Credo

I have often heard others insipidly, or, to be more kind[1], perhaps naïvely, say, "One must always be prepared."

I find this sentiment overly shortsighted and optimistic.

That a wizard should always be prepared goes without saying. What a wizard must be prepared for does not.

One must always be prepared for the worst.

To "always be prepared" implies one must be prepared for both the good and the bad.

How often have you been showered by rose petals falling from the heavens?
I have, however, been showered by arrows raining from the sky.

How often have you bathed in a pool filled with gold and gems?
I have, however, been thrown into a pit filled with burning oil.

How often have you basked in the rapturous adulation of your peers?
I have, however, been struck down by the cruel incantations of sorcerous foes.

How often have you relaxed in the loving glow of the Fae, sleeping on a bed of faerie dust?
I have, however, been enthralled and beguiled, bound in servitude by the Court of Fae.

How often have you sat down to research and had inspiration fill your mind with boundless possibilities for new incantations?
I have, however, sat down to research and had my mind imprisoned by fell grimoires, been befuddled by a miscast attempt at a new incantation, and been injured by a failed novel formulation.

How often have you set out to adventure only to uncover mysteries, magic, or treasures far beyond your expectations prior to winning your way through to your ultimate destination, ending your quest before it ever truly began?

I have, however, been thwarted before reaching my goals, found my questing to be fruitless, or discovered the attainment of my ideals to be less than worthwhile.

Being prepared for the good and the bad overly complicates life's simple equation.

Wizards must ever strive for efficiency.

Save your time and energy. Do not prepare for the good. The good won't kill you. The bad will.

Be realistic and live.[2]

Scribe's notes:

1. *A rarity for Mulogo.*
2. *At the time of this writing Mulogo has survived 3,147 years.[3]*
3. *Or so he says.[4]*
4. *At least in this regard he is doing something right... may the multiverse be saved.*

Who This Tome is For (and, by Logical Extension, Who It Is Not)

This grimoire is for wizards.

Do not try to share its secrets with others.

If I had intended for other Crafts, artisans, professions, and callings to be able to divine the contents of this text, then they would be able to divulge its mysteries.

This tome would also become as common as court gossip.[1]

Scribe's notes:

1. *Mulogo overestimates himself. And his appeal to others.[2]*
2. *For those interested, when not transcribing Mulogo's dictates or otherwise occupied by drudgery, I have added a convenient list of potential qualifying readers[3] along with associated facts and ancillary tidbits in the glossary at the end of this tome.*
3. *There are, of course, more.*

How the World Sees a Wizard

Think back to the childhood stories of your youth.

How were wizards depicted in those tales? As wise benefactors? As wondrous miracle workers? As brave adventurers? As powerful agents of transformation?

These noble themes are often far removed from reality. Do not let your view be clouded by what you wish to be, for reality is often the opposite.

If my prior admonishments have not been clear, I will now speak plainer still.

The world sees you, at best, as a means to an end.

Perhaps your wisdom is legendary. People will come to you for that wisdom. Many will want to take it.

Perhaps your knowledge is unequaled. Droves will venture to your stoop to learn at your feet. Many will want to steal it.

Perhaps your power is great. Legions will flock to you to partake of your gifts. Many will want to make them their own.

Perhaps your wealth can ransom kingdoms. Throngs will arrive at your doorstep to gain access to your riches. Many will want to build their kingdom with yours.

You are a target.

Do your best to place the world's aim elsewhere.[1]

Scribe's note:

1. *Mulogo's aim can ever be said to be his own.*

17

The Answer

This treatise is short. It could be made much longer.

Your efforts, however, will ultimately be spent much more productively elsewhere, focusing on your true purpose: learning to survive in an often hostile world.

And that, dear reader, is the true answer and ultimate purpose of wizardry. The art of survival. Everything else—knowledge, power, wisdom, insight, fame, transformation, fortune—is an added benefit (and brings with it attendant risks along the way).

Stop reading this book now and focus every fiber of your being, every drop of your will, on learning how to survive.[1]

Scribe's notes:

1. *In anticipation of your further reading, Mulogo was kind enough to continue this tome elucidating a few more points germane to wizardly survival.[2]*
2. *After 3,147 years, he still has some spare time on his hands.[3]*
3. *He also finds that it gives me something else to do.*

Types of Wizards

Generally speaking, there are three basic types of wizards:

1. The alpha wizard – These are the wizards that probably finished first in their class in wizarding school or else had a major failure in their lives that they are trying to overcome or compensate for in some way. They are frequently off to save the world, right some wrong, make the next major arcane discovery, share some revelation, or find a creative way to get themselves killed.

    Chances are, they will die sooner than they would like.[1]

2. The hermetic wizard – These are the wizards who try to remove themselves from the world, who wander with or without aim, or who spend their time in seclusion or contemplation. In most instances, these wizards hold themselves aloof but there are some that forgo seclusion in times of need to help a noble cause, disseminate wisdom, aid in important quests, or leave their cave to find someone with hedge trimmers sturdy enough to cut their beard.

    These wizards need to work on their timing.

3. The selfish wizard – These wizards care predominantly for themselves (feel free to think what you wish about me[2]) and some may be considered "evil" due to their frequent focus on their own needs and desires. Oftentimes these wizards have difficulty seeing beyond their own interests and concerns, predominantly because these are the only things that concern them (and not because they need new spectacles).

    These wizards need to open their eyes before they are blinded by what they don't see.

I would like for you to be the fourth type—the kind of wizard that survives.

Consider this grimoire my gift to you that you may become what I would like for you to be.[3]

Scribe's notes:

1. *Most people do. Mulogo being the unfortunate exception.*
2. *Mulogo is only selfish in the universal sense.*
3. *Mulogo almost always gets his way.[4]*
4. *In this case, I hope he does.[5]*
5. *There's a first time for everything.*

Choosing a Home

For centuries I tried living in a proper wizard's tower. You could say I'm stubborn.[1]

During that time, most of my efforts were spent repelling raiders (nothing says loot like a solitary wizard's tower), repairing the damage from prior attacks (and those seemed like an almost daily occurrence), or preparing for the next assault (adventurers are persistent, limitlessly poor, and more numerous than mosquitoes in the sulfurous miasma of the dankest swamp).

Then I wised up. I upgraded from a tower to a castle. Anticipating that seeing a fully guarded fastness would deter even the most brazen of rogues—thereby allowing me the luxury of arcane pursuits—I moved to my own citadel.

Apparently I had forgotten the tales of my youth. A wizard is never left alone… no matter how feared or loved.

There ensued a period of several decades where I spent more wealth and effort than I dare to admit defending a pile of rocks I cared nothing about. But I finally divined the error of my ways (at least I left the castle much more quickly than the tower!) and sought another domicile.

At last I understood my true need. I needed a home that was functional. One whose true purpose was to help ensure my survival.

Abandoning all pretense and expectation, I set up shop.[2]

Scribe's notes:

1. *You could say I agree.*
2. *And what a shop it is!*

Finding an Alternate Identity

By day, I am an accomplished pastry chef—a confectionaire extraordinaire. The subtle utilization of arcana makes my presence in the kitchen unnecessary, freeing me for other, more germane, sorcerous pursuits. I am particularly well known for my faery frostings, conjured cakes, eldritch éclairs, prophetic pastries, and charmed cookies.[1]

I can sense your feeble laughter. Your snickers and petty derision are welcome, for I am alive to appreciate the frailness of your wit.

How often have you heard of a band of stalwart adventurers raiding the fortified coffers of a pastry shop? Perhaps you have overheard many tales of mercenaries setting out to slay the vile baker? Mayhap you are considering the numerous revolts usurping the foul confectioner, giver of sweets and treats?

I thought so.

I find being a pastry chef provides the perfect cover for my wizardly activities. Bakers are expected to be up all hours "baking." I freely travel the world and beyond looking for new "recipes" and "ingredients," meeting with other "master chefs" in my journeys, in an unending effort to improve my craft. Just as tailors, cobblers, and blacksmiths employ magic to improve their wares, my more refined clientele expect their baked goods to be enhanced by a master of the magical arts—which serves my ends all the more.

If you are clever, and you will need to be to survive, there is enough ambient magic around and in use to cover your activities.

The question becomes, what craft will best facilitate your ends? Which guise will ensure your survival?

Perhaps the village you would like to live in needs a butcher or an apothecary? Perchance the local hamlet is in dire need of a coppersmith? Mayhap you fancy yourself as a glassblower? Have you ever pictured yourself as a cobbler, bowyer, artist, herbalist, bard, or stonecutter?

Choose your cover wisely. Fabricate a veil that none can penetrate. Create an illusion so banal that none care to dig deeper. Don a guise of so little outside merit or worth that no one would care to plunder your hidden riches.[2]

Scribe's notes:

1. *Mulogo's creations are the only thing about him that is sweet.*
2. *And any "hidden riches" have been plundered long ago.*

How to Deal with Neighbors

Do you want to get along with your neighbors? Do you wish to end hostility between yourself and those you choose to live among? Do you hope to live in peace with those with whom you directly or indirectly share your life and environs?

Be like them.

Be so much like them that they think you are one of them. Be so much like them that they think they know you without having to put any effort into this understanding. Be so much like them that they do not care to know you further.

Then you will have your freedom.

I have lived the opposite path.

I have shunned my neighbors. They grew to hate me.

I have put myself above my neighbors. They sought to cast me down.

I have imposed my will upon my neighbors. They fought to inflict theirs upon me.

Do not fight your community.

Win it over.[1]

Scribe's notes:

1. *Mulogo has never* won *anything.*[2]
2. *Which, I think, explains a lot.*

Protecting Yourself from Yourself

You are learning to harness the very energies of creation, the binding energies of life, and the essence of the macroverse itself.

Magic is a big deal.

Act like it.

Unfortunately, the learning curve is steep, and many fall off the cliff instead of climbing it.

Do not rush. Be patient.

Challenge yourself, but respect your current skills and abilities.

Do your best to be prepared for the worst, that you may handle the unexpected eventualities of error and failures.

You *will* make mistakes.[1] Try to live through them.[2]

Your failures are your greatest opportunities to learn.[3] Use these revelations wisely.

No matter how much you know, there is yet more to be known. Do not underestimate the power of recognizing your own limits.

If you do your best, your best will get better. With practice and effort, your skills will grow.

Give your maturation time.

Do everything you can to live long enough for your knowledge and power to flourish.

Scribe's notes:

1. *Mulogo has made all of them.*
2. *Mulogo has lived through quite a bit.*
3. *As a result, Mulogo is an unending fount of knowledge. The chances to learn from his errors, the ways to NOT be like him, are boundless.*

How to Minimize the Curiosity of Others

The subjects of your studies are wondrous, illimitably interesting. You are delving into the very nature of reality itself and learning how to manipulate it from the source to ultimate expression. The universe's highest truths are your playground, and the building blocks of your development.

There should be no end to your enthusiasm.

Don't act like it.

Be boring.

Be bland.

Be dry.

Be reserved.

Be vague.

Be uninterested.

Be unappealing.[1]

Present the countenance to the outer world of one studying the weathering patterns of shoe polish on long-abandoned footwear.

Do not draw scrutiny upon yourself.

More specifically, do not draw attention to your profession or personal matters.

Attention draws unwanted interest, takes time away from your studies and associated endeavors, and may attract unexpected dangers.

Scribe's note:

1.   *This, at least, Mulogo has mastered.*

Researching... Safely

No matter how intelligent you are, no matter how well developed your theories, no matter how advanced your magical formulae, no matter how complete your understanding, no matter what supernatural resources you have access to or summon, no one finite mind encompasses or can encompass the totality of reality.

You will fail.

You will encounter obstacles to your understanding and advancement.

Do not expect to know with certainty the outcome of your experiments or the answers they will reveal.

Be prepared, but do not overestimate yourself or your capabilities.

Be open to your limitations that you may learn.[1]

Look on your failures as successes that you may grow.[2]

But, above all, be safe.

Safety is a mindset.[4]

Before you begin researching more efficient ways to vitiate, annihilate, or discorporate matter[5], control the minds and abilities of others, or summon and manipulate ever more powerful energies and beings, consider learning to control yourself and the forces you will work with to make all your other yearnings and ambitions possible.

Focus your efforts on learning wards and shields to contain unexpected releases of powers and entities... it will happen.

Learn contingencies to counter and protect yourself and your lab when your efforts and experiments get out of control or go awry... it happens even to the best and most experienced.[6]

Learn spells and techniques to help you understand and observe your experiments before, during, and after completion... every extra iota of information can prove critical when you are seeking to push yourself forward or make a breakthrough.

Prepare your workspace with incantations and formulae to divert and control errors and alleviate dangers and mistakes. Preparation will let you live. Living will let you learn.[7]

Do everything you can to set yourself up for success because, inevitably, you will meet with failure. Failure, however, can become your greatest tool for success.[8]

Scribe's notes:

1. *Mulogo certainly is limited.*
2. *In this case, Mulogo's growth has been boundless.[3]*
3. *Yet he still has a long, long way to go.*
4. *Mulogo's mind certainly is set.*
5. *That is to say, blow things up.*
6. *And to Mulogo.*
7. *Mulogo at least has the living part down.*
8. *And, by this criteria, never has there been a more "successful" wizard than Mulogo.*

On Selecting a Name

You have persevered through your training. You are proud of your accomplishments. You are finally ready to venture out into the wide world.

Armed with a bit of caution and good sense, you might just survive.

Before you set out to conquer the multiverse, make certain you have chosen a name for yourself.[1] A proper name will help making one for yourself much easier.

Please choose a moniker that you will respond to when it is spoken.

If you don't choose a name that you will listen to, one that will turn your head when called out across a busy room, no one else will listen to it either.

How can you expect someone to listen to your name when you won't?

Scribe's notes:

1. *After a bit of research, I have discovered that Mulogo's name is derived from an alternate Ea'ae.[2]*
2. *Whether anyone will listen to it when spoken is an entirely separate concern.*

How Not to Adventure (or Be Adventuresome)

You are a wizard.

Your destiny lies in seeking and understanding the vast unknown.

Knowledge, fame, fortune, and power beckon!

The macroverse lies at your fingertips.

Leave it alone!

The world expects you to adventure.

Don't believe the hype.

Be an individual.

Go against the grain.[1]

You'll live longer.[1]

Scribe's notes:

1. *Mulogo speaks from experience.[2]*
2. *On both counts.*

Dress, Fashion, Design Aesthetic, and Otherwise How to Present Yourself

Many wizards are flamboyant. Others are flashy. Still others appear to have the fashion sense of an enchanted peacock.

This is not advisable.

You are already a target. Don't act like one.

Some wizards choose to cover themselves in cowls, hiding within the deepest recesses of cumbersome robes, burrowing beneath voluminous cloaks.

This is not recommended.

Your hands and fingers must be free to move adroitly with skill and alacrity. If you want them tangled and ineffective, bind them with ropes and be done.

Many wizards wear gruesome shrouds and veils, wreathing themselves in magical auras meant to scare, intimidate, and threaten.

This is foolish.

You are already a danger. Do not invite more.

Though you may feel that normal dress is beneath you, I implore you with every rational fiber of my being to avoid standing out. Adopt the local dress and custom.

As much as you may hate common garb, as much as you may feel this interferes with your wizardly mien, adopting normalcy may give you the chance to live.

And living may give you the chance to overcome those prejudices that forced you away from adopting sensible dress in the first place.[1]

Scribe's note:

1. *Despite Mulogo's sage advice, adopting his manner of dress is not advised. He is, in fact, rather unsightly.*

On Relationships (and Why to Avoid Them)

You are, first and foremost, bound to and responsible for yourself.

Adding another to your destiny only confuses its outcome.

Do you wish to care for others?
Become a priest or healer.

Do you wish to share your knowledge with an apprentice?
Become a sage.

Do you wish to amass great fortune?
Become a merchant.

Do you wish to control the destinies of others?
Become a publican.

Do you wish to work for the betterment of all humankind?
Reconsider your motivations for becoming a wizard.

Do you wish to share your life with another?
Do not become a wizard![1]

Scribe's note:

1. *Mulogo obviously has some deep-seated issues in this regard that are outside the scope of this tome.*

How to Manage Expectations (Particularly Your Own)

Expect the worst.[1]

Scribe's notes:

1. *Though he touched on this topic previously, Mulogo obviously had more to say here but was pulled away by patrons requesting a large custom cake order.[2]*
2. *From what I can overhear, they want the cake to be in the shape of a dragon and capable of breathing fire.[3]*
3. *Particularly at less savory guests and unwelcome relatives.[4]*
4. *I anticipate some questing will be involved to procure the requisite ingredients.[5]*
5. *Indeed. The time has come to pack our bags!*

Quests

Although you may dream of questing, of high adventure and seeking after untold rewards, keep those dreams to yourself. More often than not, you will be the object of someone else's *quest*.

A knight is in need of advice on how to slay a dragon. Who will he beseech?
A wizard.

A warrior is in need of arms and armor to defeat a foul daemon. Who does he contact?
A wizard.

A rogue is in need of enchantments to defeat a loathsome sorcerer. What agency will help his cause?
A wizard.

A magician is in search of new lore to guide his research and further his cause. What earthly power will avail him?
A wizard.

A family is in need of deliverance for an ailing relative. Who will they implore?
A wizard.

Less scrupulous but opportunistic knights, warriors, rogues, mages, and families are in need of enchantment, magical erudition, knowledge, prestige, advice, and riches to further their ends. Who will they besiege, rob, accost, threaten, imprison, or attack?
A wizard.

Find a way to thwart these dreams and avoid these aspirations and you will be well on your way to achieving your own.[1]

Scribe's notes:

1. *Evidently, Mulogo has achieved everything his heart has ever desired.*[2]
2. *If you are looking for unending opportunity to work creatively, then you have found a wonderful profession in wizardry. If you are looking for a way to achieve your own ends without becoming one for others, then your life will be a bit more complicated.*[3]
3. *Mulogo is, albeit rarely, sometimes almost right.*

On Reducing Risk (and Capitalizing on the Failure of Others)

Mayhap you have decided which piece of the universal puzzle you wish to uncover next. Perchance you have discovered a treasure trove of magical lore that you must acquire. Maybe you have discerned a wellspring of power that needs tapping. Whatever the reason, the time has come to move.

Do not move hastily.

Unless there is no alternative, do not put yourself at risk unnecessarily.

Why not let others do the heavy lifting for you?

Perhaps you know of a band of valiant adventurers looking to make a name for themselves? Give them a tip and take a portion of the reward.

Mayhap a band of stalwarts is looking for treasure but wanting a target. Provide them a goal and take a portion of the profit.

Possibly you are aware of a band of magicians looking to further themselves. Offer an aim to garner the reward.

There may be times when you need to share your aspirations to achieve your ends. There may be times when you hire out help to win your aim. There may be times when you steer rivals toward a desired goal to gauge or undermine their strength.

Whatever the reason, make certain you use all the tools available to achieve your goal without risking your own ends.

If you manipulate the situation adroitly, you may reap rewards beyond your expectation.[1]

Scribe's notes:

1. *Mulogo has reaped much. Whether he has gained is a different question.*[2]
2. *Risk little, gain much… Mulogo's life in brief.*

When NOT to Open a Treasure Chest

Really, I shouldn't have to spell this out for you, but here are some clues:

When you walk into a chamber and there are bodies lying on the floor, and particularly if they are scattered haphazardly around the chest in question, the time has come to reconsider your advancement.

If you have finally reached the treasury, especially after having battled your way through level upon level of heinous beasts, extradimensional nasties, and unwholesome henchmen, only to find it unguarded and left alone, take a moment to consider before moving onward.

In either of the above cases, if you find someone or something waiting for your arrival, and they are willing to give the chest to you, keep your hands to yourself.

If winning your way to the strongbox has been too easy, or if you feel that something is wrong or amiss, especially if you are foolish enough not to be using magic to aid in your survey of the environs, do not grant your enemies cause to question your sanity or intelligence.

In these situations, you should start by asking yourself some questions.

How much do you want the chest?

If you must have it, how much do you want it opened?

If it must be opened, when do you need it opened by?

Do you have any summoning spells at your disposal to test the best way to open it?

Are there any disposable henchmen at hand?[1]

Do you have access to any scrying spells to recreate the scene that you may better understand it?

Can you cast any divination spells that might provide you with guidance?

Are your boots in good working order so that you may run away?

Perhaps the time has come to use them.

Scribe's note:

1. *That would be me.*

On Combat (and Sometimes Avoiding It)

The fundamental forces of reality surge through your fingertips, dancing to your beck and call. Natural laws bend to your will. Your imagination guides the very expression of actuality.

Your power is unmatched.

Just because someone is charging at you waving a flaming sword does not mean you have to act like it.

A warrior rushes you in the heat of battle, brandishing a great two-handed hammer. Do you really have to call down the fires of the heavens and turn his body into an ionized cloud of superheated vapor?

Probably not.

Save your energy and effort by applying only as much force and energy as is required to survive.

How well will he be able to attack you if gravity suddenly reverses beneath his feet? If his hammer or armor suddenly weighs more than a massive cottage-sized boulder? If the air in his lungs turns to water?

An archer on the ramparts has you directly in his sights, and notches an arrow aimed at your heart. Do you bark ancient words of power to surround yourself in a seething maelstrom of magical force to deflect his arrow?

I hope not. Why draw unneeded, unwanted attention to yourself when swirling, unseen winds or a simple invisible shield will do?

A basic enchantment can freeze the water in, or on, his eyeballs, blinding him and preventing further attacks. Perhaps a slight nudge in the back or a little extra ice beneath his boots will seal his fate.

Now here's a tricky one.

A wizard begins uttering incantations that will obliterate you with a gathering of force unlike any you've ever encountered. Your wizard sight tells you she's warded against even the most powerful magics, and is likely impervious to your most potent spells.

What do you do?

Do you summon forth a swirling singularity capable of tearing apart the very fabric of space-time?

Probably not.

Do not attack her directly. She may have contingencies that counter yours. Act unexpectedly. Make careful note of the situation and respond appropriately.

She's not flying. Make the ground disappear beneath her feet. Then reseal it.

Chances are, you will be able to complete a much less complicated spell more quickly than she can conclude her masterly display of epic power. Worst case, she is distracted, you foil her casting, she loses power and the initiative and you have the chance to offer a more effective counter… like a seething cloud of grievous insects.

How well can you cast through a swarm of biting, stinging, pinching, and poisoning creepy-crawlies?

A Dwarven Dreadnaught thinks you have insulted his thane. Do you bathe him in a gout of hellish dragonfire?

I hope not.

Dreadnaughts swim in dragon flames like babies play in bathwater.

Perhaps coating him in a layer of slippery oil to hinder his forward movement and make it difficult for him to hold on to his great axe would be more advisable. You would not want his *Ur'Daena*, his axe's lament, to become your own.

Then you might have time to apologize.

Because I really hope you did not insult his thane.

A Yeren thinks you sing off-key. Do you bring an avalanche of rock, snow, and glacial ice down upon her head?

No!

Perhaps a quick silence spell will give you time to explain that you merely want singing lessons.

By the way, if you've offended a Yeren, you need licensed, professional help.

A *Caer'collas* thinks you have belittled her blade work. Do you blast her with a wall of psychic force?

I really would not recommend it.

Perhaps you should just teleport away and call it even. Then you'll have time to send her a warm note of explanation… and remorse.

A member of the Home Guard thinks you said his armor makes him look like a gigantic crystalline nightlight.

What do you do?

Aside from learning to be quiet, perhaps now would be a good time to turn invisible and hide.

Of course, if you'd studied your lessons, you would know this strategy will not work and the Guard will see through your deception.

Either ask for forgiveness or run away… quickly.

You have just told a Priest of K'un Lun that he moves like a drunken Ogre and glows like a lightning bug.

What do you do?

Nothing. This is a trick question.

You wouldn't have time to do anything (unless you were intelligent enough to have contingency spells in place and in that case you would be smart enough not to run your mouth in the first place). Besides, Priests are hard to ruffle. He probably wouldn't even raise an eyebrow.

Be creative. Use your wits. Save your true power and efforts for the adversaries that warrant them.

Chances are, you will know when they arrive. Reality usually announces their presence in one way or another… especially when the very fabric of our universe screams out in protest at their arrival.[1]

When you face dread *Anubaraëthi*, *Anubavaeri*, archfiends, and worse, you will know of what I speak.[2]

One final word: always be prepared. Surprises happen when you least expect them.

When you are capable, set up as many contingency spells for various scenarios as possible:

a.   A wizard materializes in front of you ready to vaporize you because you are known to have a first edition of *Homnobus's Guide to Great Gear*.

Have a conveniently prepared set of psychokinetic choking hands ready to throttle him and disrupt his casting along with a shield to ward against magical attacks and a spell to neutralize hostile enchantments.

You'll get to keep your first edition.

b. An assassin jumps out from the shadows behind you ready to place a poisoned blade between your shoulder blades.

Have a stoneskin spell ready to deflect her blade. Have fun with your prepared offensive response: immolate her in flames, teleport her to the nether Abyss or the vacuum between the stars, fill her gastrointestinal tract with expanding molten perlite, or any number of amusing alternatives.

She may have some rare poisonous reagents in her pockets (assuming anything is left of her to search) useful for your alchemical studies.

c. A dragon decides to use the pitch of your tower as a stoop.

Have a counter to breath weapons and magical attacks prepared along with a summoned bag of shiny objects, the more valuable the better.

You might even make a friend.

d. A daemon decides that your lab is the best doorway into the earthly plane.

Have a few banishment spells, wards against evil, protection from the supernatural, and counters to both magical, psychic and physical attack (extradimensional critters require a whole laundry list of protections) ready.

You might even be rewarded by a paladin for your efforts.

e. The list goes on^{3}... be ready.

Scribe's notes:

1. *Funny, this is how Mulogo's arrival is generally received.*
2. *For those readers keen on learning more, a helpful but incomplete list of some nasties, their associated allies, and*

abilities can be found in the reference section at the end of this treatise.

3. *As does Mulogo.*

In the Company of Wizards

Act like you are not a wizard.

Think about it.

Wizards are:

a. Often full of themselves,

b. Usually seeking to further their own motives, agendas, and ambitions,

c. Generally trying to undermine or cloud the aims of others (particularly when those aims are perceived as at odds with their own),

d. Almost always guarded, and

e. Frequently less knowledgeable than they think.

By acting unwizardly (that is to say calmly, quietly, and without pretension), you may disarm some of these common innate exclusionary tendencies. Or, better yet, you may be ignored, viewed as unthreatening, thought of as not meriting notice, or esteemed as unworthy of further consideration.

You will be amazed at what you can attain when you are underestimated.

You will be even more surprised at what you can learn when people act like you are not present.[1]

Scribe's notes:

1. *I find most people prefer to act as though Mulogo were not present.[2]*

49

2. *Wizards and non-wizards alike.*

Keeping Your Abilities and Accomplishments in Perspective

You should always aspire to do better, be better, and achieve more. This is the path of improvement for a wizard.

Though the wizarding way is dangerous, with many twists, turns, and pitfalls, you must always push forward, lest your knowledge and abilities stagnate.

To do otherwise invites your end.

To accept opens the possibility of perfection.

And this, then, is your answer.

Never look back. Look to what must be done this instant, that you may succeed and grow in the next.

Do not compare the self of this moment against one from the past, for the you of yesterday is as done and gone as an extinguished star never to be reborn. There is only the you of the future to nurture and cultivate.

And this is done by your choices and mindset each moment.

Just as you should not compare your present accomplishments with those of your past, neither should you compare your progress against that of others. Each individual is embarking on his or her own path. Where other lives lead will be determined by those individuals' choices, efforts, and fortunes.

Do not invite others' shortcomings and failings into your own.[1]

With the proper view, the right intent, correct understanding, apt choices, diligent cultivation, and an ever-deepening awareness of your self—along with its limitations and possibilities—anything is possible, least of all your betterment and survival.[3]

Scribe's notes:

1. *Mulogo has an advantage over most in that he has never invited anyone anywhere.[2]*
2. *Nor has he been invited.*
3. *It is a wonder then that Mulogo has come as far as he has.*

When the Insults Start to Fly

You are a wizard.

You are a master of words.

Hopefully, you have mastered yourself.

When the insults start to fly, remain calm. This is your chance to act, a window of response.

Chances are, whoever is insulting you has traveled a long way to do so.

Your new friend probably just wants to tell you about all the trials and tribulations he has gone through in reaching you, and to detail all the difficulties you have caused him.

Do not let him.

You can sense there is a story in his eyes as he begins to open his mouth…

Maybe your antagonist wants to tell you about how you have thwarted her plans more times than she can count.

Perchance your insultor wishes to tell you about how this will be your last instant on the material plane.

Mayhap your opponent desires to enlighten you on the hardships you have caused his allies.

Perhaps your adversary hopes to detail the innumerable losses she has incurred due to your wanton activities.

Possibly he wishes to catalogue your complete and total lack of fashion sense.

Do not give them the chance.

Their words are a gift.

Seize it.[1]

Scribe's notes:

1. *By this, Mulogo means blast them![2]*
2. *Of course, only as appropriate situationally.*

Avoiding Death (Especially Your Own!)

No, this is not another chapter on how to survive. At least not directly.

We are dying each and every moment.

Understand this truth. It is the basis for your reality and should provide one of the principal fuels to your fire and drive to move forward.

How can death be overcome?

What is waiting beyond death's door?

How can you be greater than your end that it may be overcome?

Will you accept your fate or become more?

Will you live for today or will you live forever?

These are the questions you must strive to answer. These are the answers that will determine your destiny as a wizard.[1]

Scribe's notes:

1. *Also, it really helps to avoid dying in the first place.[2]*
2. *See the rest of the volume for pointers in this regard.*

When Griffins Attack

As a wizard, you will get into trouble. Lots of trouble. Heaping loads of steaming trouble. Avalanche-prone mountains of unstably collapsing trouble.

All you can do is be prepared.

And try to relax when the excrement flies through the air like rain in the heart of a torrential summer hurricane. You'll thank me later when you keep your head and are able to respond properly to the dictates of the situation.

Your agenda will often be at odds with others. That's fine, but you had better be ready. Chances are these others, your soon-to-be pals, won't be alone. I tend to find that the agents working against your desires like to employ various beasts and critters to achieve their ends and protect their interests. The more interesting these potential adversaries are, the more power they have, the more exciting their menagerie.

You will need to study every eventuality to have some clue as to how to respond. Liches don't have your best interest at heart. Shadowkin are not looking to let you undermine their plots. Creatures from other dimensions generally don't play by the rules.

Finding and getting to your impending romantic liaison with your foes can be even more difficult than the encounter at your final rendezvous. Ea'ae's hazards are limited in comparison to some of the glorious Edens you will need to visit in your perambulations. You'll count yourself lucky if you happen upon the likes of manticores, wyverns, spectres, or revenants on your quests. In fact, your tertiary profession (after the secondary profession you have diligently chosen as an alter ego) should probably be cryptozoological tamer, because if you can't pacify or overcome the various mundane and supernatural beasts, monsters, and entities you meet along the way, you will not get very far.

This, of course, defeats the purpose of being a wizard.

Know your enemy and yourself.[1]

Know how to make your enemy a friend and make yourself better.

Scribe's notes:

1. *Knowing Mulogo: now that's a scary thought.*[2]
2. *I'm surprised he hasn't gone insane.*[3]
3. *In fact, I'd better get back to you on that...*

Allies and Whether to Buy Them

You've probably gathered by now that I am not the best source for interpersonal advice. But, for some reason unbeknownst to me, you're still reading.

Nonetheless, I will tell you this: allies are dear.

Whether bought with coin, blood, or time, you must decide whether the investment is worth the effort and risk.[1]

The decision is one you will have to live or die with.

Invest wisely.[3]

Scribe's notes:

1. *I suggest using a weighted decision matrix to determine whether developing or maintaining a given allegiance is worthwhile.[2] Calculation and additional instruction on advanced social modeling and formulae can be found in a separate volume. Please deposit all payments for said volume at the Greater Golden Bank and Trust of Tellanon, remitted to Ludaceous Vaer Mordicanum. Your tome will be delivered immediately upon receipt of payment.*
2. *It beats dusting old tomes, polishing Oedenara, and delinting Mulogo's abandoned, moth-eaten robes.*
3. *Sadly, I am not paid enough to invest.*

It's Great to Have Friends—Until They Need You

Unlike a gambler, you should be risk averse—at least as much as it is possible for a wizard to be such a thing.

Friends, like other allies, can be a great asset in times of need, whether providing support, consolation, advice, knowledge, or a much-needed blade to guard your back.

As much as a friend can be an asset, so, too, can she be a liability.

Is jeopardizing your future worth the risk?

Only you can do the calculus to determine the answer.[1]

I will, however, offer this: there's a reason most wizards live alone.[2]

Scribe's notes:

1. *See my comment in the previous chapter for help with your calculus.*
2. *And it has a lot more to do with poor hygiene, ill temperament, and lack of social grace than a glut of "risky" friendships.[3]*
3. *Of course, I am hardly one to talk.[4]*
4. *In fact, that's one of the reasons Mulogo has forbidden me from doing so.[5]*
5. *Now where's that toothbrush?*

Your Horde (and Keeping It that Way)

You have accumulated an unsurpassed fortune. Your vaults are full of gold, gems, and other metals more precious still. You have items of power and enchantment unlike those found anywhere else. You possess tomes of knowledge from other worlds, places, and times lost or as yet undiscovered by your peers. You are a repository for the unique and uncataloged.

My advice to you: put your valuables in a bank. They will be protected and insured against loss.

Do not put your life on the line for material things. Keep only what is necessary. Your efforts are best spent achieving your desired ends, not defending past accomplishments.[1]

Scribe's notes:

1. *Maybe that explains why the bakery is so wanting.[2]*
2. *Mulogo really needs to spruce up the place.*

Your Place in the World

You are the most accomplished archmage of your Age.

Kings come to you for guidance. Emperors bow to your insights. The world's greatest champions kneel before your power. Wizards of every type and tradition wish for the barest crumbs of your wisdom. The highest of priests envy the depths of your understanding.

You are at the pinnacle of your powers and the world has never before seen your like.

I beg to differ.

Whether you are in the world or not, our universe will continue on in the greater macroverse and various planes of existence. Our universe will continue to expand with its countless intergalactic clusters rotating and wandering through the void. Our galaxy will spiral about the supermassive black holes forming its luminous central cluster. The sun will rise tomorrow as its minuscule shadows, the planets of our solar system, follow in its wake. One of these specks, our world, Ea'ae, will yet revolve around the sun. The seasons will change. Plants and animals (and hopefully other wizards) will continue to grow and evolve. Magic, the energy enlivening our existence, will continue to arise from and return to the limitless fullness of emptiness, the well of potential.

You need not be a part of any of this for the macroverse to go on.

Though you are a part of the whole and a whole within its parts, without your presence existence will yet abide.

Think on this before you claim your greatness. Understand this before you proclaim the necessity of your place in the world. Internalize this truth before you avow the essentiality of your persistence within the vast stream of life dusting the barest margins of our tremendous reality.[1]

Scribe's notes:

1. *Mulogo has never said this advice pertains to himself.*[2]
2. *Especially when someone interferes with his inherent right to pontificate.*[3]
3. *But perhaps it should.*

Seizing Your Destiny (and Whether You Should Try)

This is the part of the book where I give you final words of advice.

I am going to resist the urge to do so.

Okay, maybe not.

I will reiterate.

Do everything you can to survive.

Do everything you can to better yourself. It will help you survive.

Do everything you can to learn. It will help you survive.

Do everything you can to grow. It will help you survive.

Do everything you can to adapt and evolve. It will prevent you from becoming a "crotchety old curmudgeon."[1]

By living—by doing more than just living, by thriving—you will give yourself time to find your destiny, or perhaps you will develop enough patience to let it come to you.

And you might even enjoy yourself along the way.

I know I have.

You're a wizard. You've got time. Now use it![2]

Scribe's notes:

1. He's on to me!

2. *Upon reviewing this text, Mulogo will probably cast me down into the nether realms.*[3]
3. *Please do not hold it against him.*

Glossary of Terms

People, Places, and Things

Abyss – a general name often used for extradimensional regions home to daemonic creatures of Darkness and despair. Also called *nether realms*.

Adamantium – an exceedingly strong magical metal.

Aerie – a name commonly used for the peaks and summits claimed by dragons as their homes.

Aeromancy – the study of the air and its currents, the manipulation of its energies, and the fashioning of airships.

Aerya – literally, "Light" or "air." An Elven term for the living energy of the universe. The concept of *Aerya* encompasses all forms of magical energetic expression in a single totality from the universal source to the personal creation—both chi and Yuan-chi. See also *Yuan-chi* and *chi*.

Aerya Etherum – literally, "highest air" or "highest breath." Alternatively, "first breath" or "source of breath." An Elven term for the source of the *Aerya*: the formless, boundless Void, source of limitless potential. See also *Wuji*.

Age – any extensive period of time. Typically thought of as representing one thousand years, though events of particular significance may also define its limits.

Airship – magically powered ships in as many shapes as the mind can imagine found plying the air currents and trade routes throughout Ea'ae and beyond. See also *aeromancy*.

Alchemical – Paratechnological study revolving around understanding the higher chemistries of the macroverse's functioning. Just as physical laws govern natural phenomena, and metamagical laws govern magical occurrences, alchemical laws govern the interactions between the two.

Allomorph – a being capable of taking on various shapes and guises, potentially augmenting its own intrinsic abilities, while retaining its primary core awareness, sense of self, and intelligence. The *Jira S'al Alann* are one such example.

Antientropics – the study of creating energy and adding energy back to systems, devices, and entities.

Anubaraëthi – literally, "Spawn of the Shadow," or "Shadow made manifest." A general Elven name for greater, sentient daemons. Sometimes called *Dread Lords*.

Anubavaeri – literally, "Spawn of the Flame," or "Spawn of the Fire." An Elven name for powerful daemons of flame.

Anuvaerya – literally, "Children of the Light." An Elven name for those Elves who have willingly left the bounds of the body to explore the realms of the mind and spirit. The existence of *Anuvaerya* is a closely guarded secret, known only to a few Elf-friends outside the Elven people.

Anuvatali – literally, "Children of the Dawn," or "Children of the New Morn." An Elven name for the half-Elven children of Men and Elves born on Ea'ae.

Anuvatari – literally, "Children of the Sun." An Elven name for those Elves who first came to Ea'ae.

Anuvatari'aliana– literally, "of one voice with the Children of the Sun" or "friend-kin of the Children of the Sun." An Elven name for those people of any race taken in by the Elves and taught something of their ways, or those who are trusted and respected as Elf-kin.

Archfiend – a general name for a daemon, particularly in reference to powerful daemons that have usurped dominion over lesser representatives of their own kind.

Archlich – a particularly powerful lich, often a powerful deceased practitioner of magic. See *lich*.

Archmage – a highly accomplished or powerful magician.

Archmathematics – higher order mathematics, modeling, and cognitive frameworks used in Paratechnological studies.

ARMED – Allomorphic Recombinatorial Multidimensional Extravehicular Drones. A flexible, multi-faceted, shape-changing drone system invented by Spreesprocket. Also called *sentry drones*.

Art – a calling, particularly one magical in nature.

Baera – "Brendle the All-Father" in the tongue of the Dwarves.

Baera'Dur – literally, "Brendle's bulwark" in the tongue of the Dwarves. Called *Dreadnaughts* by Men.

Baeradun – a legendary Dwarven hero known to burst into flames. Sometimes called "Burning Beard".

Beyond – a general term for other dimensions in the multiverse, often in reference to the nether realms. See *Abyss*.

Biomimetics – an area of Paratechnological research focusing on the understanding of biological functions, their governing principles, improvement, and alteration.

Blade Master – a highly proficient teacher of hand-to-hand combat in the Home Guard.

Blade Singer – see *Caer'collas*.

Bor'Banna – literally, "bearded demon." A name for the Dwarven masters of the axe, imbued by the remnants of power from Brendle's fire.

Bot – short for robot, particularly with regard to Paratechnological clockwork devices made by Tinkerers that may or may not manifest synthetic intelligence capable of independent thought.

Brendle – The All-Father. Dwarven god of the forge and, in the eyes of the Dwarves, the creator of the known universe. Called *Baera* in the tongue of the Dwarves.

Brendle's Flame – see *Brendle's Spark*.

Brendle's Spark – the remaining embers from Brendle's original flame and forge when Brendle first wrought the universe under hammer, anvil, and flame. The remaining embers even now bring forth life and magic into the universe. Also, the fires at the heart of the *Daerdaana'Duin*, the *Bor'Banna*'s highest known skill, where the exponent merges directly with Brendle's flames. Also called *Brendle's Flame*. An analogue to *Aerya* and Yuan-chi in Dwarven cosmology.

Brendle's Tears – the finest of Dwarven ales. Reputed to be so wondrous and flavorful that Brendle himself cries tears of joy and amazement with each sip.

The Cabal –A sinister alliance of dark mages, fallen Priests, extradimensional beings, and other creatures of might bent on not only domination but power. Known by many other names, including the Order of the Lidded Eye, the Fallen, the Light Fallen, the Order of the Burning Eye, and the Order of the Hooded Gaze. Called Liúxīng Làngrén by the Priests of K'un Lun. Often symbolized by a blazing sigil of a closed eye.

Caer'collas – a Q'sharian blade master. Often called *Blade Singers* by those who watch their masterful interplay of magic and blade work.

Champion of Light – a general honorific for those who have earned great esteem fighting the forces of Darkness. Also, a title for one of great accomplishment within the Dalaren Ka.

Chi – Qi; breath, air, or vapor of particular significance in Taoism and Eastern medicine. From a Taoist perspective, the chi is the vital energy or life force that enlivens and pervades all things. Chi gung—chi kung or qigong—are exercises to build and strengthen chi flow. Along with shen and ching, one of the Three Treasures essential to human life. Chi is a less subtle and refined form of the Yuan-chi, the universal potential. The fire that does not burn.

Clockwork – a general name for a particular branch or type of Paratechnology focusing on magically animated contraptions of any shape, size, and function, often resembling machines and robots but not limited to any specific shape. A particular specialty of Gnomish Paratechnological Tinkerers.

Common – see *Common Tongue*.

Common Tongue – a universal language used across Ea'ae to facilitate nonmagical communication. Also called *Common*.

Craft – higher magical skills. An umbrella term inclusive of various branches of magic including unique talents and abilities native to particular races, guilds, and tribes.

DADD – Dwarves Against Drunk Dragons. Also, Dragons Against Drunk Dwarves.

Daemon – a general name for extradimensional creatures with hostile intent or for those otherworldly creatures that feed and prey upon the energies of the living. Also called *infernals*.

Daerdaana'Duin – literally, "to become the heart of fire" or "to become the heart of the forge". One of the highest skills of the *Bor'Banna*, wherein the practitioner wreaths himself in the flames of Brendle's forge, becoming a direct manifestation of Brendle's power and one with its heat, energy, and vitality. In times of old, these warriors cloaked themselves in flames, striking down foes directly with Brendle's might. See *Brendle's Spark*.

Daer'Duin – literally, 'heart of fire' or 'heart of the forge'. Given Dwarven name for Slate Flintforge.

Dagron Grey Beard – a famous Dwarven *Dur'kazak* of old.

Darkness – a general term for those beings opposed to the Light and Life it engenders and who would subvert, pervert, or otherwise mar Its presence and manifestation. Also a general term for the corruption of the energy of life, the Light, itself.

Delving – a general name for any Dwarven city or outpost. See also *undermount*.

Deur Spricken Sprack – Gnomish for "the Omnispark." See also *Phlogiston* and *Omnispark*.

Djazoth Al'Zann – a world conquering antihero, cultivator of rare orchids, and collector of stuffed bunnies.

Doerdaana'Duin – literally, "the dance of the heart of fire" or "to dance in the heart of the forge". One form of Dwarven axe work known for its fluid strikes and counters, commonly used by particularly adept *Bor'Banna*.

Dragonflight – a group of dragons living and moving together.

Dragons – along with the *Aeryn D'al*, one of the oldest races of Ea'ae. Steeped in magic and power, dragons are feared by all who cross their path. As complex as they are storied, dragons are as diverse as their characters and can wield power rivaled only by the gods themselves.

Drake – dragon.

Dread Lord – a general name for higher-order, more powerful daemons granted intelligence and power far beyond their peers. Called *Anubaraëthi*, Children of the Shadow, by Elves.

Dreadnaught – a Dwarven warrior specializing in heavy combat. Utilizing enchanted, rune-etched full plate armor along with two-handed axes, hammers, and maces, Dreadnaughts earn their place at the fore of the battlefield by fighting against the most implacable foes. Famous as much for their rallying battle cries and songs—along with their fear-inducing chants and dirges—as for their blades. Called *Baera'Dur* in the tongue of Dwarves.

Drothman – a famous Dwarven hero.

Druids – protectors of the wilds, guardians of nature, and lovers of freedom. First students of the *Indural*.

Dunédâne – literally, "deep delver". Name for the Dwarves among their own kind and the Karadüm.

Duraeleon – "The Light Bringer", bane of Adrael the Black, ancient axe of Ithilieon. Wielded by Slate Flintforge.

Durden – literally, "valiant heart". A Dwarven rune that serves to protect against fear and indecision when properly enchanted.

Durin – a famous Dwarven hero from times of yore.

Dur'kazak – literally, "fire shaper." A Dwarven master smith skilled in the art and craft of metallurgy, elemental magics, and rune crafting known as *Karaduen*.

Dwarves – along with Elves, Gnomes, and Men, one of the four most prominent races on Ea'ae. Dwarves are short, hearty, and solidly built, and are known for their ability to work metal. They excel at reading the earth and mining. Their keen knowledge of metals and runes allows for the creation of powerful works of Craft. Also called *Dunédâne*.

Ea'ae – "The world." Home to magical creatures and races of many shapes, cultures, and forms. Also, an exceptional book series.

EGAD – see the *Every Gnome's Anti-Intelligence Device*.

Elf-kin – Those people of any race taken in by the Elves and taught something of their ways. Sometimes called Elf-friends or *Anuvatari'aliana* in the tongue of the Elves.

Elves – a fey race at home among the trees and dells of Ea'ae. Elves are a race of great Craft and knowledge that made peace with the land long before the coming of Men and Dwarves and many other sentient races. It is said that magic is the lifeblood of the Elves. Often called Lords of the Wood or Tree Singers by Men, although not all Elves are indeed *Iyela*. Those Elves on Ea'ae are the *Anuvatari*.

The Enemy – Ur'Daus, the Darkness between dimensions. Also known as the Creeping Shadow, Destroyer of Light, the Umbral Lord, the Devourer of Worlds, among many other names and curses.

ENNIS – see *Epistemic Noetic Numenetic Integrating Summator*.

Epistemic Noetic Numenetic Integrating Summator – a multifunctional Gnomish device with capabilities ranging from measurement and systematic evaluation of phenomena, data analysis, computation, and communication to independent reasoning, learning aid, thought transference, and toothbrush. Also called *ENNIS* for short.

Every Gnome's Anti-Intelligence Device – a Paratechnological defensive system, suitable for espionage, surveillance, and camouflage, added to items ranging in size from personal armor to airships. The Every Gnome's Anti-Intelligence Device replicates the surrounding environmental variables and superimposes them over the object protected by the defensive system, rendering it indistinguishable from its surroundings. Sometimes referred to as EGAD or, more specifically and to add to the general air of confusion and embellishment around Gnomish devices, as the Every Gnome's Anti-Intelligence Clandestine Apparatus version 3.1, Corvette Class.

Evility – the expression of the primacy of an individual's needs and interests before the needs and interests of the group or placing the needs of one society ahead of another. The opposite of civility.

Extrabiology – the extension and expansion of biological systems, processes, and representations.

Face of the Mountain – a Dwarven term for an unreadable, stoic visage, as unchanging and unyielding as the mountain rock, particularly suited for floundering and confounding others.

Festival of the Clans – a large gathering of Dwarven clans filled with celebrations, competitions, reunions, feasting, drinking, sharing of lore, addressing of grievances, and forging of alliances.

Fiersayne – the brood and broodmates of Cersaegian.

Flashwhistle Boomblaster – A Gnomish Paratechnologist known for his particularly explosive zest for discovery and knack with incendiary devices.

Fria al'Othra – literally, "eyes of true vision." An Elven term for the universal perspective of the *Iyela*.

Früea – a Dwarven master artisan. The skills of a *Früea* range from creating fine jewelry and ornamentation to complex magical and mechanical artifices.

FTP – faster than physics. Gnomish Paratechnological communications system that allows communications faster than allowed by the (Non)Standard Model of physics.

Future history – the Paratechnological study of outcomes and possibilities.

GastroGnome – Gnomish lover of fine foods.

Gnomes – a race of short stature but of broad mind known for their creativity, imagination, and Paratechnological aptitude. Originators of Paratechnology, famed Tinkerers, often unable to leave well enough alone. Distant relatives of Dwarves.

Gnomeproof – a Dwarven colloquialism for foolproof.

Gnomosphere – Gnomish term for the noosphere.

GPE – Gnomish Protective Equipment.

Günda – literally, "Dwarf excrement." An Orcish curse.

Henosis – a theurgical practice whose ultimate aim is unification with and expression of the Divine Light.

Homeworld – planet of origin or primary habitation for a race, species, or group.

Hröthe – literally, "divine healing". A Dwarven *Karaduen* offering a one-time boon of healing from a grievous or debilitating wound.

Human – see *humanity*. A general name for an individual member of any of the sentient races on Ea'ae.

Humanity – a general name for all humanoid races on Ea'ae. Men, Dwarves, Gnomes, *Indural,* and other sentient races of Ea'ae are included under this broad description. As a naturalized race, Elves, too, are considered part of Humanity, although they are genetically distinct from the other humanoid races.

Hürn – literally, "evil's bane". A Dwarven rune used for protection from evil.

Idealized engineering – the practical translation of Paratechnological ideas to actuality.

Illdrassil – literally, "Spire of the Heavens" or "Tree of Heaven" in the Old Tongue of Men. The home of the Council, Tellanon's ruling body and the Home Guard. A vast repository of magical energies that empowers the city in the sky.

Indural – one trained in the magic, lore, and woodcraft of the forest giants.

Infernal – a daemon.

Iyela – an Elven lorekeeper, wonder worker, tree singer, and shaper. Known for their ability to commune with the spirit of trees and request the boon of their heartwood, the *Aeryn Sh'al*. Called Tree Singers by Men.

Jira S'al Alann – literally, "People of the Imagining". A race of changelings able to shift their guise and abilities depending upon their magical development and attunement. See also *allomorph*.

Karaduen – a Dwarven word meaning "Light's ward" or "Light's seal." Special Dwarven runes and symbols often employed by *Dur'Kazak* and *Kor'Dannan* in the crafting of artifacts and the creation of spells and enchantments.

Kazzak – literally, "marks of honor" in the tongue of the Dwarves. Symbols, tokens, and items of repute woven into a *Bor'Banna*'s beard as badges of honor and accomplishment. Also common among other Dwarves.

Khuerkanna – a famous Dwarven general known for his triumphant last stand against the Orcs and their allies in the Battle of the Broken Blade.

Kiloboulder – a Gnomish unit of force, energy output, and weight.

Koerdian Cave Bear – a species of gigantic cave bear particularly respected by Dwarves for their strength, perseverance, and indomitable spirit.

Kor'Dannan – Dwarven Priests of Brendle given the keeping and wisdom of his fires, Brendle's Spark. Fierce warriors equally adept at healing and providing succor.

Lich – undead beings sustained by twisted magical energies.

Life – all living beings taken as a whole.

The Light – the ambient energy of the universe; the energy of Life enlivening all of existence. Considered holy, sacred, and heavenly. See also *Aerya*, *chi*, ching, dalare, *Deur Spricken Sprack*, *Omnispark*, *Phlogiston*, shen, *Brendle's Spark*, and *Yuan-chi*.

Loess – literally, "Heaven's shielding". A protective Dwarven rune meant for use against supernatural forces.

Ludaceous Vaer Mordicanum – wondrous scribe, scholar, and luminary. One of the greatest intellects of his or any generation.[1]

Mulogo's note:

1. *Or so he thinks.*

Luerdan – literally, "troll dung" in the tongue of the Dwarves.

Macrocosmos – see *macroverse*.

Macroverse – the totality of multi-dimensional existence, inclusive of all planes, alternate universes, and extradimensional regions. See *multiverse*. Also megacosm or macrocosmos.

Magic – the translation of the possible into the actual, the imagined into the real. The three primary components of magical practice are often understood as: *belief*, faith that an individual can take an active part in universal creation; *intent* (or will), the shaping of this belief to guide in creation; and *imagination*, the vision or desired outcome made possible by belief and shaped by intent.

The wellspring of magic is universal energy. Depending upon the tradition, this source is known as Yuan-chi, Brendle's Spark, Phlogiston and the Omnispark, *Aerya*, and Light, among others. This universal energy is often understood as the source and fuel of life, the chi. Sometimes broken into greater and lesser magics referencing the differentiation between the universal source energy—Yuan-chi, Phlogiston, *Aerya*, Light, and celestial or divine magics—and the intrinsic ambient energies of life: the chi.

See also *Yuan-chi*, *chi*, *Brendle's Spark*, *Phlogiston* and *Omnispark*, *Aerya*, and *the Light*.

Major and Minor Shielding – a complex combination of spells serving to protect the recipient from arcane damage and hostile spells (the Major Shield); while also guarding against physical damage, impacts, blows, cuts, and the like (the Minor Shield).

Mauguer – a Dwarven brewmaster. Of their many secret arts, brewing Brendle's Tears is the most closely guarded.

Megacosm – see *multiverse* or *macroverse*.

Men – the youngest and most prolific race of Ea'ae. Native flexibility and intuitiveness allows Men to excel in many fields, progressing quickly through their chosen arts.

Metamagics – the study of magic in and of itself, its laws, and governing principles.

Mithril – a particularly light, yet strong, magical metal.

Möerak – a skilled Dwarven miner with an uncanny ability to uncover valuable veins of ore, minerals, and gems.

Mulogo – accomplished wizard known for many magical theories and refinements as well as drafting *Mulogo's Treatise on Wizardry*.[2]

Scribe's note:

> 2. *A* cynical old curmudgeon who fancies himself something of a wizard.

Multimodal computational panlogic – the theory of structured and unstructured reasoning, rational and irrational decision-making, and generally making things up.

Multiverse – the entirety of multidimensional space, inclusive of alternate universes, planes, and dimensions. Also macroverse and megacosm.

Mysteries – a general name for types or classes of magic.

Nether realms – extradimensional planes home to infernals and other fiendish creatures. See *Abyss*.

New Unified Mental-Energetic Noesis – NUMEN. A synthetic Paratechnological being of great mental and physical capacity, able to take on many shapes, forms, and functions. An extension of the Paratechnology developed in the TAMERS units without need of an operator, as the NUMEN is guided by its own intelligence. Also, a play on words among Paratechnologists for their magical-technological creations that may one day supersede them.

Noeldri – literally, "flowing water". A Dwarven rune granting grace and agility both physically and mentally.

Noerlag[3] – a double-bladed great axe of high renown. Chosen weapon of Urdaen Doomhammer. Called *Fellblade* by the Dwarves. Called *Spinetickler* by the Orcs. Composer of texts of Dwarven lore. Of absolutely and most assuredly no relation to Duraeleon.

Dwarf's Note:

   3.   *A lyin' cur with a tongue as sharp as its treacherous blade.*

Noosphere – the realm of the mind, the collective consciousness, or the sphere of thought. A general name for the metamagical plane allowing for the shared existence and interaction both within and between various synthetic intelligences. A Paratechnological creation of the highest order. Also references the sphere of thought, mind, or knowledge itself. Also called the *Gnomosphere*.

Notional physics – the Paratechnological study of the higher (and lower) laws of the universe, the greater macroverse, and its various subsets.

Nüaerblun – literally, "dragon dung" in the tongue of the Dwarves. Often used as a Dwarven insult.

Nüaer'Daer – literally, "life's heart." A Dwarven term for dragons.

Nüaer'Duin – literally, "dragon fire" or "life's fire" in the tongue of the Dwarves. Among the Dwarves, dragon fire is respected for its magical properties and power so like the heat of Brendle's forge.

NUMEN – see *New Unified Mental-Energetic Noesis*.

Occlusion – a Paratechnologist known for his overzealous shaving habits.

Occlusion's razor – a simple axiom arrived at by Occlusion after much trial, error, and many, many cuts… getting the most for the least.

Oedenara – literally, "daemon's heart." A crystalline gem, found at the heart of some daemons, that has powerful magical properties and is of much practical use.

Omnicron – a Paratechnological device capable of generating and sustaining immersive, non-virtual actualities.

Omnispark – Gnomish conception of the ignited or expressed source of life unending, ever-changing and evolving, fueled by Phlogiston. *Deur Spricken Sprack* in Gnomish. Also called Yuan-chi, *magic*, *Aerya*, *Brendle's Spark*, and *the Light*, among other terms, by other races.

Orcs – a large and prolific evil race spread through the wilds and caverns of Ea'ae. Orcs are strong, aggressive, and full of guile, a race of warriors and shaman. Working in league with Trolls and Ogres, Orcs often lead their slower witted brethren on the field of battle.

Paladin – a holy warrior dedicated to and empowered by the Light. Paladins are vanquishers of evil, banishers of the unholy, adjudicators and arbiters, healers and almsmen. Many variants exist, some dedicated to particular deities and powerful entities, each with different talents, specialties, and ethos. The Dalaren Ka are one such group.

Parapsychology – the magical study of the mind, its features, moods, states, and manifestations.

Paratechnology – literally, "beyond technology." The study of making the imagined real and actualizing the impossible. The art and science of applied magic and magical technologies. Paratechnological apprehension is shared across many races, however the Gnomes' natural curiosity and creativity have brought Paratechnological expertise to its current refined state and have helped to spread its knowledge throughout the cosmos.

Phlogiston – called *Deur Spricken Sprack* in the tongue of Gnomes. In Gnomish reckoning, the invisible spark of life pervading the universe akin to an invisible metastate of gaseous energetic conductance. Once ignited, Phlogiston fuels all life as the Omnispark. When manipulated by will, the Phlogiston gives rise to magic. Also called Yuan-chi, *magic*, *Aerya*, *Brendle's Spark*, and *the Light*, among other terms, by other races and traditions.

Phylactery – an amulet, charm, or safeguard against harm or danger. Also, a vessel for relics.

Plane – one of many distinct layers of existence in the larger macro or multiverse. Often synonymous with universe or dimension.

Pocket dimension – a miniature space or reality created expressly for a specific purpose. In the case of the myriad pocket dimensions of Tellanon, these represent miniature universes intimately connected to Tellanon itself, extending its breadth and depth. More often, pocket dimensions are used to extend space within a given region—for example, to make the space within a bag or room larger.

Pocket fairy – small, often cantankerous fairies given to taking up residence in Gnomish pockets.

Powers – beings of great might, often extradimensional in origin.

Priest – one who has been accepted fully into the Order of the K'un Lun. See *Priest of K'un Lun*.

Priest of K'un Lun – an Order of mystics dedicated to the practice of various esoteric and martial traditions found nowhere else on Ea'ae. The way of the Priest is geared toward continual transformation and development within and without through the evolving practice of internal alchemy.

Priest of Maeth Onai – an order of magicians from the cold Northlands that practices a unique blend of mundane and divine magics whereby divine energies are channeled to perform traditional and inimitable spells.

Projection – a general term for a multi-dimensional representation of an object, such as a magical hologram or depiction. Also a reference to life-like, immersive news feeds displaying current happenings and items of worth.

Psion – a being gifted mentally and psychically.

Psionics – psychic mental powers and abilities as expressed by a psion.

Rakshasha – Sanskrit for demon. A race of powerful feline daemonic sorcerers in league with the Cabal.

Saedeus Moerdencanum – warlock, dictator, despot, and all-around not so nice guy. Saedeus's empire spread far and wide across several galaxies and planes through a pernicious combination of fell necromantic sorceries and high technologies. Saedeus's reign of intergalactic terror was ended when his conquests disrupted the vegetable supply of a particularly enterprising group of Gnomes with an inordinate fondness for rutabagas.

SAVERS – see *Self Actuated Variable Emergency Response System*.

Sceaduwulf – literally, "shadow wolf." A spectral wolf.

Schema – The patterning, diagramming, representation, and planning of Paratechnological devices, theorems, strategies, and abstractions.

Scierdyas – literally, "spectral dragons." Energetic beings very similar in appearance to dragons summoned from the unholy nether realms of the darkest abysms.

Self-Actuated Variable Emergency Response System – a Paratechnological clockwork emergency response bot of Gnomish invention, capable of independently responding to, assessing, and reacting to multiple life-threatening situations. Called *SAVERS* for short.

Sentry drones – a general name for Paratechnological defensive drones. See also *ARMED*.

Shade – a nebulous creature of Darkness.

Shadow – a general term for creatures of Darkness and their ilk. Those opposed to the energy of Life in all its manifestations and who seek to subvert, pervert, consume, or otherwise destroy the Light in all its manifold expressions.

Shadowkin – a general term for creatures of Darkness. See *Shadow*.

Shaur'Daus – literally, a "Stalker of Darkness" in the tongue of the Dracodaerans. Draconic warriors wreathed in the fires of heaven that do battle against the creatures of Darkness across the cosmos and beyond.

Shen Po – master of the void palm, one of the fallen founding fathers of the K'un Lun, member of the Cabal, and one time teacher of Master Wei.

Shiny – a highly sought after, much admired quality in Paratechnology. Shiny is a very complex term with many shades of meaning. Except when its meaning is simple. Typically understood as desirable or bright and highly reflective; or the state of being such. Discussions of shiny are never dull.

Skael – a people of nomadic traders who travel the skies in airships plying their wares.

Spreesprocket Goldpulley – Gnomish Paratechnologist and humble writer of many insightful texts.

Südaer – a Dwarven lorekeeper and magician.

Super sack – a magical Gnomish bottomless bag. Super sacks are often cluttered, disorganized, and very difficult to retrieve items from, especially within a short, highly critical period of time.

Suprachemistry – the study of how magical and nonmagical systems, compounds, elements, entities, and components interact, react, behave, change, and develop.

Synthetic intelligence – a Paratechnological term for the sentience resulting from the merger of two different intelligences. Typically, one intelligence is natural and the other is artificial, one is organic and the other is disembodied or a metamagical complex arising from technical sophistication, or one intelligence is formed explicitly to merge with and augment another. Far different from the Abstract and Construct's relationship with Citizens, for example, wherein one intelligence serves another directly and indirectly, synthetic intelligences are the result of a complete union between two disparate awarenesses, the resulting union having complete access to the knowledge and capabilities of both. Most typically, one intelligence is created explicitly to merge with and augment another, extending the field of sentient consciousness into directions and dimensions limited only by the imagination.

Also a reference to any created intelligence.

Taerris'thule – literally, "old home." Formerly a religious city and home to the seal of Eldre'gheu. Sometimes referred to as the City of the Fallen Gods.

TAMERS – see *Transmorphic Actionable Multidimensional Exo-Robotic System.*

Tellanon – literally, "Heaven's Landing" in the Old Tongue of Men. A spectacular floating island city in the sky, a center of commerce and diplomacy, and a starting point for both interstellar and interdimensional travel. Home of Illdrassil, the Home Guard, and Paratechnologists on Ea'ae.

Thane – traditional leader of a Dwarven clan.

Tinkerers – Paratechnologists focusing on clockwork devices melding magic and technology in forms often resembling complex mechanical devices. Most often associated with Gnomish Paratechnologists due to their strong imaginative mechanical tendencies.

Transmorphic Actionable Multidimensional Exo-Robotic System – A multi-functional, transforming exoarmor system created by Spreesprocket. Also known as TAMERS.

Traveling – teleportation or any other form of instantaneous travel ,whether inter- or intra-dimensional.

The Umbral Lord – see *the Enemy* or *Ur'Daus*.

Undermount – a general name for any Dwarven city or a Dwarven occupied region. Typically located in the bedrock beneath mountains. Undermounts are composed of Dwarven fastnesses and attendant halls and byways that grow within the roots of the hills. Also called delvings, though delvings are typically smaller in scale.

Ungar – literally, "earthen might". A Dwarven rune granting physical strength and endurance.

Urdaea – Urdaen's granddaughter.

Urdaen "Flamebeard" Doomhammer – Dwarven hero and inspiration for many a tome and tale. Most fortunate wielder of Noerlag.

Ur'Daena – literally, "the axe's lament." The uniquely Dwarven art of the axe. Many styles and forms are known, each generally ascribed to a specific family, clan, or thanedom. Variations in styles—from the use of great two-handed war axes taller than a man suited to the openness of the battlefield, to forms of double-bladed combat better suited to the close quarters of a mineshaft—are all practiced with distinctly Dwarven fervor.

When practiced by a master, a *Bor'Banna*, these styles rely as much on channeling the remnants of Brendle's original creation magic through the axe as they do on physical prowess for their efficacy. When wielded by a true master, the axe of the *Bor'Banna* is said to glow with the light and heat of Brendle's original forge.

Ur'Daus – literally, "The Darkness." Also known as the Enemy, the Creeping Shadow, the Devourer of Worlds, the Umbral Lord, the Great Devourer, and many others. A fathomless Light consuming Darkness trapped between dimensions in Ages long past.

Vanduen – literally, "divine regeneration". A Dwarven *Karaduen* that enhances healing capacities, speeding recovery and repair from exhaustion and injury.

Vöer – troll, in the tongue of the Dwarves.

Vöerdan – literally, "Troll saliva or spittle." A Dwarven insult.

Void – the wellspring of creation. The limitless potential underlying all existence.

Vradek – Orcish gruel made from ground bones simmered in blood.

Vyaera – literally, "wanderers along the path." An Elven term for those sharing the same path, quest, purpose, or journey.

War of Shadows – one name for the first war with the Cabal and their dark allies, waged on Ea'ae in the distant past.

Worgs – massive wolves used by Orcs as mounts in lieu of horses.

Wyrm – an ancient or powerful dragon.

Yerens – a noble race of yeti-like creatures. Singers of the worldsong. Called the Shapers of the True Song, Shapers, and Singers.

Younglings – a common name for Dwarven children.

Yuan-chi – the primordial energy, the inherent unrealized potential, of the universe; the celestial or divine *chi*.

About the Author

Joe is a minor Initiate into the Lesser Mysteries, capable of summoning forth minor vaporous eructations, weak charms (presumably feeble attempts at wit), and underappreciated conjurations generally in the form of acrylic on canvas (although he aspires to watercolor).

Including influences such as Shunryu Suzuki, Tolkien, Krishnamurti, Iain M. Banks, Laozi, Stephen R. Donaldson, Philip Kapleau, Raymond E. Feist, Edward O. Wilson, Dan Simmons, and David Bohm, Joe creates existential fantasy filled with rich worlds, concepts, stories, and ideas.

Joe holds an advanced degree in environmental management from Duke University where he also studied religion with a focus on meditative, experiential, and transformative traditions.

When not at play with his family, he enjoys reading, writing, and relaxation. When he can, Joe also practices various martial traditions in which he has attained the victim level of proficiency.

In addition to *Mulogo's Treatise on Wizardry*, Joe is also the author of *Everygnome's Guide to Paratechnology, Nemesis – A Good Guide for Bad Guys, Confessions of an Angry Dwarf*, and the *Chronicles of the Fists* trilogy.

Author's Final Note

I hope you enjoyed reading this book as much as I did writing it.

Whether these words transported you to another place, one you enjoyed wholeheartedly, or pushed you away without lasting impression, I would welcome your fair and honest review[1] (good, bad, or indifferent) of my book wherever you may choose.

If you truly did appreciate this book, feel free to spread the word to your friends, family, and random acquaintances. I would also love for you to visit me at either my website at www.josephjbailey.com or on my Facebook Author's Page.

If you would like to learn about future book releases, please consider signing up for my book announcement newsletter.

Many thanks and happy reading!

Joseph J. Bailey

Scribe's notes:

1.   *Mulogo does not condone reviews.*

www.ingramcontent.com/pod-product-compliance
Lightning Source LLC
Chambersburg PA
CBHW030150200626
46812CB00016B/1781